Moon
Loon

Sandy Ferguson Fuller

TAYLOR TRADE PUBLISHING
Lanham • New York • Boulder • Toronto • Plymouth, UK

**For Johnny,
and for Spring,
with love,
forever.**

Published by Taylor Trade Publishing
An imprint of The Rowman & Littlefield Publishing Group, Inc.
4501 Forbes Boulevard, Suite 200, Lanham, Maryland 20706
http://www.rlpgtrade.com

Estover Road, Plymouth PL6 7PY, United Kingdom

Distributed by National Book Network

British Library Cataloguing in Publication Information Available

Library of Congress Cataloging-in-Publication Data Available

ISBN 978-1-58979-453-5 (cloth : alk. paper)
ISBN 978-1-58979-455-9 (paper : alk. paper)
ISBN 978-1-58979-454-2 (electronic)

∞™ The paper used in this publication meets the minimum requirements of American National Standard for Information Sciences—Permanence of Paper for Printed Library Materials, ANSI/NISO Z39.48-1992.

Printed in China

CPSIA tracking information
Shenzhen, Guangdong, China
January 2010
Cohort: Batch 1

Moon

Loon.

**Loon beneath the silver moon,
when I hear your haunting cry
it always makes me wonder…** *why?*

Moon Loon,
late at night, dark or bright,
I wake
and hear you wailing.

Are you lonely?

Is that why?

I know that loons will mate for life.

Where is your wife?

Moon Loon,

don't cry.

Moon Loon,
sometimes you arrive at dawn . . .
    softly, like the white-tailed fawn.

I try to follow, but not too near,
    or I will hear the fear
        filling your tremolo voice.

Moon Loon,

   sometimes you swim by at noon
     beneath the golden sun.

   Like the raccoon,
     I've watched you fish.

**Oh, how I wish
that we could dive together,**

just for fun.

**Moon Loon,
in the afternoon,
there's no sound but crickets peeping.**

Are you sleeping?

But then a *hoot*…

hoot…

hoot…

Will we soon be meeting?

Just as you come into view,
I hear your yodel greeting.

**Moon Loon,
is it true what they say?**

**In winter, when I'm far away,
will your beautiful feathers turn to gray?**

**Will you fly off to a distant bay
to stay until the spring?**

**Moon Loon,
in the cold of winter,
will you still sing?**

Moon Loon,
in the icy wind
don't be lonely ...

You're my friend.

Just listen.

Wait for a spell.

Keep safe.

Be well.

Before too long,
it will be time again for summer's song.

June will be here very soon,
and I'll come back
to share your tune.

I hope you find a mate,
Moon Loon.

Good night.